D1327752

Contents

A catalogue record for this book is available from the British Library.

First edition

Published by Ladybird Books Ltd Loughborough Leicestershire UK
Ladybird Books Inc Auburn Maine 04210 USA
Printed in England

ANIMAL
stories for
Under Fives

by JOAN STIMSON

illustrated by
COLIN and MOIRA MACLEAN

Ladybird Books

Brown Bear's visit

Brown Bear had just finished breakfast.

"That was horrible," he grumbled. "What's next?"

"Next," said Mum, "you can go to the playground while I tidy up."

Brown Bear began to grizzle.

"Same old friends, same old slide. It wouldn't be so bad if we had a climbing frame."

Brown Bear was grouchy all day. Then, when he got home, Mum sent him off to the waterfall... for a shower!

Brown Bear came back damp and grumpy. He grumbled as he gobbled his supper. He grizzled as he snuggled into bed. Mum tucked him in and told him a story.

"AAAAH! That WAS boring," he yawned. And fell asleep.

Next morning Brown Bear had a visitor. It was his cousin from across the mountain.

"Can you come to play?" he asked. "Mum says you can stay the night."

Brown Bear barely said goodbye to his mum. He didn't wave to his friends on the slide. He just jogged along beside his cousin and asked what they were going to do first.

"First," said Brown Bear's cousin, "I'll show you our climbing frame. Then I'll take you home... to meet the twins."

Brown Bear couldn't wait to try the climbing frame.

"It's easy," said his cousin. "Just watch me and my friends."

But Brown Bear had never turned a somersault before. He fell off and bumped his nose!

Brown Bear's cousin didn't seem to notice. He carried on clambering with his friends until it was time to go home.

Brown Bear cheered up at the thought of food. But Auntie was all behind.

"Those twins," she cried, "are ALWAYS under my feet."

But then she had a brainwave.

"Why don't you big bears take the little ones to the river? You can bath them for me. And bath yourselves at the same time."

"Why can't we go to the waterfall?" cried Brown Bear. "I don't like rivers."

"Because we don't have one," said Auntie, simply. She began to tidy up.

As soon as they reached the river, the twins squirted Brown Bear and his cousin. Then, just when it was time to go home, they rolled on the bank and got all dirty again.

Brown Bear had NEVER been so cross or so hungry.

"Here we are at last," said Auntie. But, as soon as she brought in supper, the other bears swooped like vultures.

Brown Bear's tummy was still rumbling
when he went to bed. It was so dark he
couldn't even see his cousin.

"Can I have a story?" he called out.

But Auntie was already snoring. And so
were all the other bears.

The next day Brown Bear's cousin led him
along the track. He pointed in the direction
of Brown Bear's home.

"Look," he said. "Your mum's coming to
meet you."

Brown Bear barely said goodbye to his cousin. He bounded along the track as fast as his legs would carry him.

"It IS good to see you, Brown Bear," said Mum. "Now what would you like to do first?"

Brown Bear nestled up to Mum. Then he put his nose in the air and breathed in the sweet smells of home.

"LOVELY FRIENDS, LOVELY SLIDE, LOVELY WATERFALL, LOVELY MEALS AND LOVELY STORIES!" he cried.

"And I want to do it ALL first!"

Hippo hiccups

Hic, said the hippo,
I don't know what I've done.
I've only played, *hic*, in the mud
And lazed, *hic*, in the sun.

Hic, said the hippo,
However can I eat?
I'm, *hic*, *hic*, hiccing from my nose
Right down, *hic*, to my feet.

Hic, said the hippo,
I'll stand, *hic*, on my head.
I'll MAKE those hiccups better
Oh, *hic*... they're worse instead!

Hic, said the hippo,
I'll try a tiny drink.
Perhaps some, *hic*, *hic*, water
Will make my hiccups shrink.

Ssssh, said the hippo,
Is it too soon to say?
I think the worst is over
Hooray! Hip, *hic*, hooray!

The singing lion

The little lion loved singing.
But he couldn't sing
in tune!

"Shall we have a singsong?"
he asked his mum.
But Mum couldn't face it.
"Not now, dear, I'm
starting one of my
headaches."

The little lion wandered off, humming under his breath.

"Shall we have a singsong?" he asked the giraffe.

The giraffe bent her long neck to listen. But she soon shot back up again.

"Not now, thank you," she whispered. "I'm getting a sore throat."

"Help!" thought the little lion. "I hope I don't lose MY voice."

"Shall we have a singsong?" he asked the zebra. "It goes like this..."

But the zebra was already into his stride. "Not now," he called. "I must go for a run."

All the other animals suddenly disappeared, too. The little lion couldn't understand it. But then he came across an explorer and a film crew.

"Shall we have a singsong?" roared the little lion.

But the explorer and his film crew panicked. They dropped their megaphone and fled.

From then on there was pandemonium on the plain.

"SHALL WE HAVE A SINGSONG?" bellowed the little lion.

It was SUCH fun singing through the megaphone.

At last a crafty old snake decided to brave the din. She persuaded the little lion to follow her to a lonely cave.

"In you go," hissed the snake. "Someone inside wants to meet you."

The little lion stepped forward nervously.

"It's very dark," he whispered.

"That's because my friend is shy," replied the snake. "He doesn't like to be seen. But he does like a singsong!"

The little lion rushed inside and sang at the top of his voice. And to his joy another voice joined in. It even knew all the same songs.

The little lion spent many happy hours singing in the cave with his friend. The other animals decided not to tell him that it was really an echo of his own voice.

So once more there was peace on the plain.

A surprise for a tortoise

Nimble and Leaf were chatting about birthdays. Leaf had begun the conversation because it was going to be HER birthday very soon.

"This year," she said proudly, "I shall be ONE HUNDRED years old. And I want to do something special!"

"Leave things to me," said Nimble (who was a nippy ninety-three). "I'll fix you the tortoise treat of a lifetime."

Nimble thought long and hard about Leaf's birthday. She asked the other animals for suggestions. But no one had any bright ideas.

By the night before Leaf's birthday Nimble was desperate. She tossed and turned in her shell. Then, just before midnight, she thought of the PERFECT birthday surprise.

"I've got it! I've got it!" cried Nimble and scuttled off to tell Jumbo. But Jumbo didn't want to wake up. He nestled deeper into the undergrowth and sucked his trunk.

Next Nimble went to see Chimp. She found him burying bananas at the bottom of his tree. But, when Chimp heard the rustle of tiny feet, he fell flat on his back. And started snoring.

Last Nimble went looking for Parrot. Parrot was wide awake, all right. But he was gazing at his reflection in the lake. And practising his best joke.

Nimble couldn't get a word in edgeways.

"Bother!" she cried. "I shall have to catch them all in the morning."

At first light Nimble explained her plan to Jumbo.

"A SURPRISE FOR A TORTOISE!" he boomed. "I'm much too high and mighty for that."

"Fair enough," said Nimble. Then she added politely, "I do hope I didn't disturb you last night... when you were sucking your trunk."

"WAIT!" Jumbo didn't want the other animals to know he still sucked his trunk so he agreed to help.

Next Nimble went to see Chimp.

"What a lot of fuss about nothing!" he cried. "And, anyway, I shall be busy."

"Of course," said Nimble politely. "You'll be busy... burying bananas."

"WAIT!" Chimp didn't want the other animals to know about his secret hoard so he agreed to help.

Nimble found Parrot by the lake.

"A treat, a treat," he squawked. "I'll give YOU a treat!"

"Yes, please," said Nimble politely. "Will you tell me that joke... the one you were practising last night?"

"WAIT!" Parrot didn't want the other animals to think him vain so he agreed to help, too.

When Leaf woke up on her birthday, everything was ready.

"Close your eyes," said Nimble. "Here comes your surprise."

"Is it a big surprise?" asked Leaf.

"Quite big," said Nimble. "You can open your eyes now."

As Leaf looked up, Jumbo strode forwards. On his back were Chimp and Parrot.

Leaf looked confused. "What is it?" she asked.

"It's a RIDE ON A JUMBO," said Jumbo proudly. "I'm going to take you on the trip of a lifetime."

"But, what if I fall off?" asked Leaf. "And how will I get up there?"

"That's MY job!" cried Chimp. "I'll carry you onto Jumbo's back. And then I'll be your seat belt."

"And I'M going to be your guide to all the sights!" squawked Parrot. He tapped his beak with a knowing air.

"Did you enjoy it?" asked Nimble when they all came back.

"It was a WONDERFUL birthday surprise!"
cried Leaf. Then she looked shyly at her
friend.

"Do you know any whales or dolphins,
Nimble? Because next year I should like to
take a CRUISE!"

25

Which flamingo?

The flamingoes lined up
In a long, long row.
There was something important
They needed to know.

"Oh please, Mr Toucan,
Do tell us, please.
Which of us here has
The knobbliest knees?"

The toucan looked up
And scratched his chin,
For how could a toucan
Know where to begin?

There were so many knobbles
On so many knees.
He began to feel hot
In spite of the breeze.

The flamingoes grew restless.
"This is no fun.
For heaven's sake, Toucan
Tell us who's won."

So Toucan spoke up
And prayed he would please.
"You've ALL got the best and
The knobbliest knees!"

Flop learns to swim

Flop, the penguin, was nervous. It was time for his first swimming lesson.

"Hurry up!" called Dad at the top of his voice. "We don't want to be late."

"Hey! What about breakfast?" cried Flop. "We don't want to be hungry either."

"Just a small one," said Dad. "Too much food will give you cramp."

Down by the sea Flop got cold feet. He tugged at Dad's flipper.

"The water's FFFFREEZING!" said Flop. "Let's go home for more breakfast."

Dad took no notice. "The first thing to learn about swimming," he began, "is to relax."

But Flop didn't feel relaxed. He felt cold and wobbly.

"What if I can't do it, Dad?" he whispered. "Everyone will laugh."

Just then a group of young penguins rushed past him.

"Watch this, Flop," they cried.

One by one the penguins dived into the sea. And covered Flop with spray.

"Brrrr! Brrrr!" Flop's beak
began to chatter.

"Please, Dad," said Flop. "I want to go home."

But Dad was beginning to enjoy himself. "Never mind THEM," he said. "Watch ME."

Flop shivered miserably on the shore.

"Splish, DEEP, splosh, BREATHS." Dad began his demonstration.

"Splish, CHIN, splosh, UP," he gasped. "Now YOU try, Flop."

Flop took a deep breath and waded towards Dad. But then he tripped and fell beak first into the water.

"HELP! HELP!" yelled Flop. "I'M DROWNING."

Dad scooped Flop out of the water. He patted him firmly on the back.

Flop choked and spluttered.

"I don't want to do any more swimming today," he whispered.

Now it was Dad's turn to choke and splutter.

"Call THAT swimming?" he bellowed. "Now, for heaven's sake, Flop, please CONCENTRATE!"

Flop tried harder and harder to swim. Dad tried harder and harder to teach him. But the harder Dad tried, the louder he shouted.

"Please, Dad," said Flop. "I'm not DEAF. I just can't swim."

Dad gave a huge sigh and one last demonstration. But it was no good. Flop just couldn't do it.

Dad waddled back to the shore. He sat down with a plop... the picture of disappointment.

Just at that moment another father arrived in the bay. His young daughter was swimming strongly beside him.

Flop's dad groaned and put his head in his flippers.

Flop felt so sorry for his father that he did a very brave thing.

He bobbed carefully out to sea until the water reached right up to his beak. Then he swam along... with one foot on the bottom.

"Look at me! Look at me!" quavered Flop.

"WELL DONE, FLOP!" beamed Dad. He started to strut along the shore.

"Well done!" beamed the other dad. Then he took a closer look at Flop's father.

"Why, it's old Shortie!" he boomed.
"I haven't seen you since those TERRIBLE
swimming lessons. Our fathers nearly
deafened us. Don't you remember? In the
end we went along with one foot on the
bottom... just to keep them happy!"

"AHEM, AHEM, AHEM!" For some reason
Flop's dad couldn't stop coughing.

Flop was fascinated. Fancy that penguin
calling his dad "Shortie." And fancy Dad
swimming along with HIS foot on the
bottom.

Flop began to feel relaxed. He wriggled his toes in the water and gave a little chortle. Then, all of a sudden, he gave a great WHOOP of delight.

"I'M SWIMMING! I'M SWIMMING!" he cried.

And, as he shouted, Flop flipped onto his back and waved both feet in the air... just to prove it!

Crocodiles do climb trees

"Don't do that, Mum," said Snappy.
"Crocodiles aren't meant to dance. They're
meant to slither and be menacing."

But Snappy's mum didn't want to slither.
She didn't feel menacing.

"Slow, slow, quick quick, slow." Snappy's
mum waltzed up to a clump of trees and put
a flower behind her ear.

Snappy groaned. "Leave it out, Mum. What
if any of my friends see you?"

Snappy's mum didn't mind WHO saw her.
She carried on dancing all afternoon. Then,
instead of slithering in a nice, menacing sort
of way, she shot up the nearest tree.

"Mum, Mum," shrieked Snappy. "CROCODILES DON'T CLIMB TREES!"

"This one does," said Mum. "It makes me feel good. I like the view."

37

Snappy stomped off to the river bank and sulked.

"Come on in!" cried a voice from the water. "It's a lovely day for a dip."

Snappy slithered down the bank. He liked the look of this new friend.

"He's just my sort of croc," thought Snappy. And, before he knew it, Snappy had invited him over... the next afternoon.

All night long Snappy worried and wriggled. However could he make his mum behave in front of his new friend?

Snappy swung into action at the crack of dawn.

"Wake up, Mum!" he cried. "We'll dance all morning. Then you'll be too tired to dance this afternoon!"

"Slow, slow, quick quick, slow." Snappy and Mum danced themselves dizzy.

"Let's have lunch in that tree," cried Snappy at last. "Then you won't need a climb later!"

"PHEW!" Snappy got Mum back on the ground just in time.

"I think I hear someone," he said. "Now, please remember... CROCODILES DON'T CLIMB TREES!"

"THIS ONE DOES!" boomed a friendly voice.

Snappy couldn't believe his ears. It was his new friend's mum.

"Slow, slow, quick quick, slow!" She was dancing along in front of her son to show him the way.

Snappy's new friend groaned and blushed. But Snappy gave his widest grin.

"We're going swimming," he called over his shoulder.

But, of course, Snappy's mum didn't hear him. She was too busy showing HER new friend the view... from her favourite treetop!

41

Teamwork

Two leopards were wearing
A terrible frown.
They wriggled and jiggled
And jumped up and down.

They twisted, INSISTED,
"I CAN count my spots,"
Then tumbled and grumbled,
"I'm tied up in knots."

They growled and they scowled,
They hadn't a clue.
Then all of a sudden,
They knew what to do.

They bounced and announced
And shook their great paws,
"You can count my spots...
And I will count yours!"